SUSAN WILLIS is an author living in Birtley, Co-Durham. She has ten novels, seven novellas, and a collection of short reads.

Writing Psychological Suspense and Cosy-Crime novels with strong, lovable North East characters, is her passion.

Susan also writes stories for Woman's Weekly magazine.

All her work is available on amazon here: https://amzn.to/2S5UBc8

Copyright c 2025 by Susan Willis All Rights reserved. No part of this novel may be reproduced in any form by any means, electronic or mechanical (including but not limited to the Internet, photocopying, recording), or stored in a database or retrieval system, without prior written permission from the author. This includes sharing any part of the work online.

Susan Willis assets her moral right as the author of this work in accordance with the Copyright, Designs and Patent Act 1988.

The characters, premises, and events in this book are fictitious. Names, characters, and plots are a product of the author's imagination. Any similarity to real persons, living or dead, is coincidental and not intended by the author.

Also By Susan Willis:

Where Have They Gone
A Year of Short Stories
Payback at the Guest House
Confession is Good or the Soul
Intriguing Journeys at Christmas
Joseph is Missing
Death at the Caravan Park
The Curious Casefiles
Magazine Stories from the North East
Christmas Shambles in York
Clive's Christmas Crusades
The Christmas Tasters
The Guest for Christmas Lunch
The Man Who Loved Women
Dark Room Secrets
His Wife's Secret
The Bartlett Family Secrets
Northern Bake Off
You've Got Cake
A Business Affair
Is He Having an Affair
NO, CHEF, I Won't!

Chapter one

Deirdre

I'd felt frozen to the core hurrying home from work in the first week of January. Freezing sleet bombarded my face and a strong wind made it impossible to keep my umbrella up for shelter. It was only a few minutes' walk up the road from the bus stop to my flat, but tonight it seemed like miles. Finally, I slotted my key into the front door and hurried through into the hall, dropped my bags onto the wood floor, and shook the wet from my coat.

Now, with the central heating on high and the log burner creating a warm glow in the lounge I'm snug and toasty. I wriggle my toes in the thick socks I knitted last winter in a Fair Isle Shetland wool. Watching the local news on TV, I pick up my knitting to while away another winter's night. I smile remembering how on New Year's Day I had decided to knit my way into 2025.

Knitting is something I have always done, a hobby that my foster mam, Sheila, had taught me in my teens. When my friends from school were out in nightclubs and pubs learning the art of mixing alcohol and drugs, I'd been more than content to stay home and learn a new knitting pattern.

I'm knitting the last sleeve on an Aran sweater for my friend, Gill at work. She's not exactly a close friend, more of a cross between a good acquaintance and an alley when I need one. Which nowadays seems to be on a regular occurrence. I work as part of the assistant's team in the coroner's office. There are four of us in our section and we all report into Gill who is assistant to the coroner himself.

I hold up the pink woollen sleeve and admire the intricate cable work I've achieved. I imagine pretty, blonde Gill with her elven face and figure wearing the sweater. I'm sure a size ten will be a perfect fit and I know that pink is her favourite colour. This would never suit me because at six foot and wearing a size eight shoe, I'm too big and ungainly to suit the colour pink. I am more of a brown, grey or black woman.

Gill often admires my knitted sweaters in the office, so I'm sure she will love this surprise gift on her birthday. Last week, she had fingered the rib on my blue Nordic style jumper and said, 'Ah, Deirdre, that's another lovely sweater.'

I'd smiled back and gushed my thanks.

'It feels so soft and cosy,' she'd said. 'Which is just what we need at this time of year.'

I smile at the memory then slot one of the needles snugly under my arm into position. I begin to knit the first row from a sixteen-row pattern. I chant out the stitches, knit three, purl six and repeat to the end.

I love the control of knitting patterns. When you adhere to the pattern with the correct wool, size and shaping it always makes a perfect garment. There are no variables. Which cannot be said for many other things in life.

The pink sweater is simply perfect. I glow with the satisfaction of making something that is correct and structured. It is similar to how my life is now with no room for failures and mistakes. There have been enough of them in the past and I frown.

At nine o'clock, I get up and wander through the open plan lounge into the kitchen to make a cup of herbal tea. While I wait for the kettle to boil, I look around the simple clean lines of my home and sigh with pleasure. It's what Sheila would call a trendy modern flat and the complete opposite to our old house near Durham Cathedral.

Here, I have light wood floors with big scatter cushions, smooth leather furniture and cream painted walls. I love the look which an interior designer helped to complete.

When I'd moved into the flat last year and shown my photographs to everyone at work, they'd flattered me with compliments. Well, everyone except Hannah. She is the youngest team member and often makes snidey comments.

'God, if you can afford to live there, I don't know why you keep coming back to work every day,' Hannah had said with a snort. 'You must be mad!'

I'd shrugged my shoulders. Mainly because she had been right. I didn't need to work any longer. Last year, I won, Set for Life, lottery draw of £10K a month for the rest of my life. However, I decided to continue working because I would miss the company of Gill and the rest of the team. I'd grimaced knowing Hannah was probably the only person I wouldn't miss.

Trying to make my reply humorous, I'd said, 'Oh, but I'd miss your happy smiling face every day, Hannah.'

She'd shaken her head and looked me up and down then tutted loudly. 'Jeez, some people get everything handed to them in life,' she groaned. 'I mean, what more could you ask for?'

I had taken a deep breath and stared at this beautiful young girl who moaned incessantly about her large interfering family. However, from previous conversations, I knew how loving and supportive her family were. I clicked the photographs closed on my mobile unable to think of another witty reply. I'd wanted to rage at her that she didn't how lucky she was but had bitten my lip.

I'd shuffled my big brogues on the linoleum and mumbled, 'I would ask for a family.'

We'd been in the café queuing for lunch, and I wasn't sure if she'd heard my reply, but Gill had stepped in between us. She had moved

Hannah swiftly forwards with her tray while I hung back and gulped down tears. I'd whispered under my breath, 'And to know who I am.'

I potter back to the sofa, sipping my tea before slumping down into the soft comfortable cushions. There is only Gill at work who knows that I am a foundling. None of the team know anything about my background. And that's the way I like it. I'm a private person and my childhood has always been a taboo subject which is never up for discussion.

I sigh and sip my tea. Foundling is such a strange word. Ever since Sheila explained what had happened to me as a baby, I've thought the word found sounded like a dusty old book or a weather-beaten handbag in a lost property depot. Although that's not where I was found. I was rescued from a telephone box outside a Chinese takeaway in Durham City.

Which strangely enough isn't far from this new block of apartments where I now live on the outskirts of the city. So, in a way I have returned to where I was originally found. I've been back to where the telephone box used to stand but of course it was removed years ago and now there's just a square slab in the pavement.

I've stood outside what was the take-a-way, now a modern sandwich bar and looked around the street hoping for some type of thunderbolt or revelation. In my dreams, my mother hurries back to rescue me, but I've woken in a cold sweat knowing this was a fantasy. All the same, my mind often drags me back there, wondering if there is a connection between me and that particular street. Or did my mother simply choose the street at random. Whichever it was, I hate her with a passion that on some days feels uncontrollable.

Apparently, I was named, Deirdre after the Irish nurse who cared for me in hospital until Sheila and Jack were judged ideal foster parents. When I was fourteen, I'd looked at the Foundling Museum website in London and read this description. 'Foundling' is an historic term applied to children, usually babies, that have been abandoned by parents and discovered and cared for by others. There are currently twenty foundlings every year in the UK.

I think of my parents now and sigh. I couldn't have been cared for any better by Sheila and Jack until I was nineteen when they had been killed in a car accident. I've been alone ever since.

Chapter Two

Deirdre

I'm sitting at my desk in the corner of our small office. It's an old but beautiful building with the disadvantage of cramped rooms which are too hot in the summer and very cold in the winter. The old cranky radiator in the corner doesn't give out much heat therefore the warm sweaters I knit are beneficial.

It's Monday morning and I'm planning to give Gill her pink sweater at lunchtime. I smile anticipating the look of surprise on her face. I open a spread sheet on my computer to record data that Gill needs by eleven this morning. It's a monthly record of the forms we have issued to release bodies to relatives for funeral arrangements. I'd done most of the entries on Friday therefore it should only take me an hour to tidy up the document.

I'm half-listening to the general chatter between the other three women about their weekend shenanigans. Hannah is telling everyone about her Saturday night dancing to a new song in a club with her friends. What she wore, her perfect make-up and hair, and how most men couldn't keep their eyes off her.

Shallow is the word that Sheila would have used to describe her. And I know she is right. The older woman, Linda teases her about the way she is bragging, and Hannah twists a huffy look onto her face. This is usually a prelude to her lashing out and verbally attacking someone. Which is very often me.

I keep my eyes down fixed on my keyboard and take a deep breath awaiting the onslaught. Gill is at a meeting so the adjoining door to her office is closed. No back up there, I think and feel my stomach twist.

Linda doesn't like to get involved in any of the office politics, therefore I know she won't take my side in an altercation. The other two women who started work in the team as strangers have apparently fallen for each other and are hoping to marry next year. Good luck to them, I say. If you've been lucky enough to meet someone in life that makes you happy then go for it.

Gill often says, 'Those two are joined at the hip but can type and work faster than the whole team put together!'

Gill is a great believer in playing to one's strengths. And Hannah? Well, Gill reckons she is an IT wizard who keeps our systems and processes in tip top condition.

Hannah leans forwards now over her keyboard towards Linda. Their desks face each other, and she whispers something. Her shoulders are hunched in a green tight-fit jacket. In the past I know she has called me the weirdo, and I'm sure I've just heard her utter those same words.

I see Hannah's reflection in the small window next to my desk. I spin around in my chair and glare at her back. My heart starts to thump, and I grind my back teeth. Who the hell does she think she is calling me names? I feel like I'm back in senior school. I never stood up for myself back then but now as a thirty-five-year-old woman, I have had enough.

The words explode from my mouth. 'Well,' I hiss. 'If I am weird, it's because of cruel bullies like you that have tormented me all of my life!'

There is a deafening silence. Linda has her head down staring at the mouse and the other two women are in the furthermost corner so might not have even heard. I reach under the desk and grab my handbag then march off down the corridor to the cafe.

***

I sit alone sipping a hot cup of tea trying to work through the anger and frustration whirling around in my mind. I take slow and steady deep breaths until my heartbeat slows. I wipe my lips and mouth with a tissue. Am I weird? Or is it like Sheila used to say, 'You're just a little bit different to everyone else.'

Well, if I am weird, it's not my fault. And at my age I reckon I'm too old to change now. It's my bloody mother's fault whoever she was. What kind of a woman would leave a baby in a telephone box? Was she out of her mind? Did my father not want to know me either? I mean, if my mother were unbalanced surely my father could have looked after me until she was better. Or, at least kept me safe. Sheila reckons that he might not have known, and my mother was probably a very young single girl.

There again, if I'd been in that situation, I would have at least contacted the hospital to get my baby back when I was well again. Even if it had taken years. I would have been desperate to know what happened to my child and if she was being well looked after. I'd have worried in case my baby had caught a chill in the cold draughty phone box, after all it had been the 16th December.

Sheila had made excuses and said, 'But you were well wrapped up in thick cosy blankets, Deirdre.'

But this hadn't satisfied my torment. What if I had thrown the blankets aside? Had I been crying because I was hungry without milk, or had she breast fed me? Apparently, there had been a bottle of warm milk tucked into the crook of my arm, so I suppose at least she hadn't wanted me to starve to death. And, seemingly, I hadn't been alone long enough for the milk to cool.

Over the years, I've tried to find some empathy for this woman, my so-called mother, but I can't. I hate her. I know the way I've turned out is because of what she did. When you're a foundling, you get used to rejection on all levels. And I feel that I've never been accepted anywhere, apart from Sheila and Jack, of course. Although they were very good and kind to me, there was no demonstrations of love towards me. No cuddles an hugs. Or if there were I can't remember them.

If I'd had a loving, caring mother and been part of a big family with brother and sisters, I could have been a much better person. I wouldn't have had all the pent-up frustrations and endless unanswered questions that most days drive me crazy. I'd once heard Jack say that I was growing up with a humungous chip on my shoulder. And maybe, he was right. Some days it feels like a crater that I carry around which has made a dent in my shoulder So, yes, Hannah, I reckon I am a weirdo now.

It is days like today when I wonder if I should finish work and be a lady of leisure. Which seems to be what everyone thinks I should become. However, I sigh, there is only so much leisure time I could fill with activities every day. I've thought about learning more craftwork, sewing, dressmaking, or embroidery, but don't feel confident enough in my talents.

People cry, why not go on a cruise ship and see the world, but I'm not a great traveller and know I would be seasick. And I hate flying.

When I was twenty, I'd been engaged to a man called, Jimmy. Sheila had described him, as quite a catch. There'd been a sneer around her mouth as she'd said the words and I had wondered whether she'd meant that he was a great find for me? Upon this, I hadn't been too sure.

Jimmy had badgered me for months because he wanted us to fly over to Paris to celebrate our engagement. I'd relented but had been physically sick with nerves for the whole two-hour flight. Although I enjoyed the sights of the Eiffel Tower and Arc de Triomphe, I'd worried every moment in fear of the flight home.

When we had arrived back in Durham he'd cried, 'You've spoilt the lovely weekend I had planned!'

I'd muttered, 'I'm sorry, but I didn't want to go in the first place.'

And that really had been the beginning of the end for us as a couple.

I sigh and wash my face in the ladies room then slump back to the office.

Gill has returned from her meeting and calls me though to her office. Apparently, Linda has told her about Hannah's cruel comment and how I'd retaliated.

She leans forwards across her desk with her hands clasped together.

'Are you okay, Deirdre?'

A week winter sun streams though the window and glistens off her large diamond engagement ring. I look at it with longing. The diamond must be four times the size of the engagement ring Jimmy had slid onto my finger. Of course, I've put so much weight on now the ring won't even slide up past my knuckle but it lies proudly in my jewellery box, just to remind me that at one time in my life, someone did care.

I remember how he'd shouted, 'Deirdre, you're completely obsessed about this foundling business.'

And I'd yelled back, 'Jimmy, this is not some business. This is about me. It's about my life!'

He'd grumbled. 'But it's all you think and talk about.'

After the arguments I would try and put it to the back of my mind especially when I was with him. But it didn't work. I couldn't let go of the hurt and anger towards my mother. Eventually, he'd walked away. And there had been a large part of me that was glad so I could wallow in my memories without interruption and interference.

'Deirdre?'

I realise I've wandered off in my thoughts and shake myself. 'Oh yeah,' I mumble. 'I'm fine.'

Gill raises a fine pencilled eyebrow. 'Well, I've spoken to Hannah about making inappropriate comments in the office and I'm hoping to see an improvement in her behaviour,' she says. 'I thought it was just a few sarcastic jibes, but Linda has told me the extent of her bullying. You should have told me, Deirdre?'

I hunch my shoulders and stare past her out of the window. 'I learnt at school that challenging bullies only makes the situation worse.'

The tension in my body begins to ebb and my face warms in gratitude for Gill's friendly defence. 'I don't think Hannah is a bad kid. She's just got a lot to learn in life, like us all I suppose.'

'Okay,' she says. 'But please let me know if it continues and I'll consult with HR.'

I smile back and nod. Gill is one of these fifty-year-old super women with a big family and an amazing husband. For years she's been a foster mother taking in children on short term placements and totally understands my need to trace my ancestry and background. Gill helped me to arrange the saliva DNA test and place my details into an online data base which is critical to the process of tracing parents and siblings.

It's as though she can read my mind now, when she asks, 'Is there any news from the database?'

I shake my head. 'Nope, I'm still patiently waiting for some type of contact,' I say, then sigh. 'I suppose it's a case of where, do you find someone who doesn't want to be found?'

Chapter Three

Mary

The arthritis in my ankle is aching this morning as I press the old pedal on my sewing machine. Now at the age of seventy, I should be slowing down but dressmaking is something I've done all my life, and it's hard to stop. I've sat in the bay window of this small cottage at my sewing machine every day for as long as I can remember. I watch all my neighbours in the village pass by the window and wave every day as I sew one garment after another.

I am hoping to finish the sides of a dress I'm making for my neighbour, Elsie. She has a wedding invitation for the spring and although I'd started making her dress before Christmas, I am struggling to meet the deadline. Well, it's her deadline, not mine.

I'm confident that I'll have the dress ready for the March wedding, but yesterday Elsie had stressed, 'Oh, Mary, I need a fitting as soon as possible to show my daughter in London.'

I'd reassured her. 'Elsie, I won't disappoint you and the dress will be ready. I've never once let anyone down.'

I frown knowing this is not strictly true. During my lifetime there is only one person that I have let down and that is my daughter. I bite my lip. I failed her on a monumental scale when I abandoned her.

I overlock the sides of the material and cringe at the horror of those days. It's something that even now I cannot bear to think about. I sigh and shake my head. Did I have any rational thoughts in my mind that day at all?

I'd given birth in a strange house with my aunt holding my hand. Two days later I had been plonked onto a train home from Scotland cradling a howling baby. A woman in the carriage had rocked her until she'd stopped crying but when I'd tried to do the same my baby cried even louder. I'd been terrified. I had panicked and knew that I wouldn't be able to cope with her.

Carefully, I'd placed her in the bag inside the telephone box and prayed someone would take her away to a safe place. Far away from me. However, even in my frantic state of mind, I'd waited on the corner of the street until a woman opened the door to the telephone box. The woman had a friendly kind face and she'd cried out at her discovery. Foolishly, I'd hoped this woman would know how to stop her crying because I had failed. I'd howled in terror and ran away.

For years after I was discharged from St. Margaret's hospital, I tortured myself daily and the nightmares had seemed never-ending. Where was she? What happened to her? Was she being cared for? In my dreams nobody rescued her from the phone box and months later she was found as a skeleton in the blankets. I would sit bolt upright in bed screaming.

I wipe tears from my cheek now and leave the material on the side of the sewing machine then potter through to the kitchen. I swallow some painkillers to ease the ache in my ankle and take tea and biscuits back to the lounge. I sip the hot tea in my fireside chair then lift my foot up onto a stool and close my eyes waiting for the painkillers to take effect.

I'd known nothing more about my baby until my dad died ten years ago when I had cleared out his belongings and sorted his paperwork. My mam had died following a stroke three years previous, so it was left to me to make the funeral arrangements. In an old miner's tin, I'd found a newspaper from 1985. In capital letters emblazoned across the front page it read, BABY FOUND IN TELEPHONE BOX IN DURHAM CITY!

I remember how shocked I had been that dad knew about my baby. For years after she was born, I'd thought only Mam had known.

'You can't stay here and have the baby,' she'd shouted. 'You'll have to go up to Edinburgh. You can stay with my sister and have it up there where no one knows us. I can't have your disgrace as a single mother living in this village.'

I had slumped down onto the floor next to Dad's old bed. My hands had shaken so much I hadn't been able to hold the newspaper, so I spread it out onto the carpet. Tears had streamed down my cheeks, and I'd wiped my face twice before I managed to read the smaller print. I gulped at the words which answered the questions I'd tortured myself with for over twenty years.

My baby had been safe and well in Dryburn hospital. She had a name which I'd rolled around my tongue and repeated aloud into the silent room. They had called her, Deirdre after an Irish nurse who had cared for her. I'd smiled at the fact that my mam had been half Irish and a staunch catholic.

I open my eyes now and see old Ted pass by the window then wave. I know everyone in this village, and everyone knows me. It is a small mining village near Durham. Of course, since the closure of the mines the community is vastly changed. The miner's cottages are filled with elderly people like myself and have become retirement homes. There are very few young people in the area now. But it is all I know. It is where Dad met my mam, and I was born.

I wriggle my toes and open the Velcro on the front of my slippers as the ache begins to ease. I finish my tea and much through two custard cream biscuits. I usually just have one biscuit a day, but I'm allowing myself a few little treats now.

Last week in the hospital the doctor had said, 'The results of your scan are not good, Mary. It has shown us what we've previously talked about, I'm afraid.'

The young nurse who'd stood next to him in the small consulting room had taken my hand and squeezed it tightly. I'd seen the concern in her eyes because I had been alone in the room. I supposed the nurses were used to having relatives with their patients to support them through difficult times.

'It's okay, pet,' I'd said. 'It's just what I was expecting. There's no need to fret yourself, I'll be fine.'

And I have been. I have taken the news in my stride and am prepared for what is ahead.

I look over at the red sewing machine and sigh. It had been a Christmas gift from him. Christmas has never been a good time for me as it holds too many painful memories. It had been twelve days before Christmas when Deirdre was born, and it had been two weeks before Christmas when I'd met him. He had been the only man I ever loved. His name, Michael still sticks in my throat even after all these years.

My mam used to stress the word, *him!* As though, she couldn't bear to say his name either. I know I should get back up and finish the stitches on the hem of Elsie's dress, but I slump back into the chair letting the memories flood through my mind.

When Dad was made redundant at the pit, I had been told to find some work. I'd protested to Mam. 'But I make good money dressmaking?'

'I know, Mary, but that is on a now and then basis,' she'd said. 'We need a regular weekly wage coming in now your dad is out of work for when we get older.'

I had wanted to ask her why she couldn't find work, but I'd been too scared of her rebuff. Therefore, I had started work in the canteen at Durham University although they called it a refectory. The first few weeks had been hard because I wasn't used to mixing and socialising with big groups of different people. I'd complained to mam. 'I feel nervous every morning on the bus going into Durham.'

'Oh,' she'd said. 'You'll be fine once you get used to it every day.'

Eventually, I got used to the four days a week away from the cottage. It had been early autumn when Michael had stopped me one day in the refectory. I'd been wiping empty tables after the lunch time rush, and he'd spilled a plastic cup of orange juice. 'Sorry to be a pest but could you wipe up the mess I've made.'

I'd looked up into the biggest brown eyes I had ever seen. He'd had a name badge pinned to his pale blue shirt which read, Professor Michael Davidson. I'd been gobsmacked and quickly cleaned the table by the time he returned with two cups of juice.

He'd grinned. 'Here, sit down and have a drink with me.'

I'd felt my knees buckle slightly and glanced over my shoulder to make sure the supervisor wasn't in sight then slid onto the bench opposite him. And it had been as simple as that.

He'd told me how beautiful my grey eyes and brown shiny hair were and lavished compliments upon me until I was completely spellbound. We started to meet in Durham, and he had taken me for lovely meals in restaurants introducing foods I didn't know existed. On my birthday he presented me with the red sewing machine which I think he'd bought second hand. But it didn't matter, I loved it. I read every book he recommended from the library and to use Mam's phrase, 'Michael had completely swept me off my feet.'

Those were probably the kindest words mam had said about our affair. The cruellest words had been, 'He must have been clapping his bloody hands to find a thirty-five-year-old virgin without an inch of common sense in her head!'

It had been three months into our relationship when I found out he was married with two small children.

'But I thought you knew,' he'd said and kissed down the side of my neck. I had dumbly shaken my head. I'd also known that as awful as the situation was it didn't matter. If he kept making love to me on the back seat of his car I wouldn't object. And he did just that. It was all I lived for.

When I missed my period, I honestly thought it was an early menopause because my monthlies had been hit and miss. When the doctor confirmed I was pregnant I'd been horrified at first. But after a few days when I had become accustomed to the idea, I'd felt excited about having a child of my own.

I'd tried to ignore Mam's cruel taunts. 'This usually happens to seventeen-year-old girls who don't know any better, you idiot!!'

Two weeks after I'd told Michael about the baby he suddenly transferred to another university in Wales, and I never heard another word from him.

I reach over now to the small coffee table in front of the fire and pick up the letter and information that arrived last week. Deirdre has requested contact and although I have been avoiding the decision, I know it must be done.

I pick up a pen and notepad then write.

Hello, Deirdre,

I'm not sure how to start this note but all I know is that not one day has gone by that I haven't thought about you. I can make excuses about why I left you, but they will seem trivial to you. All I can say is that at the time they were very real to me in my life.

I'd like to see you if possible but will totally understand if you don't want to meet.

Your mother, Mary.

Chapter Four

Deirdre

Gill had loved her sweater when I'd given it to her before leaving the office on Monday and had proudly worn it the next day with black trousers. Everyone who came into the office complimented her and when she'd explained that I'd knitted the sweater it made me glow with satisfaction. Linda had asked me to knit one for her sister to which I've agreed.

Even Hannah had admired my skill and made pleasant comments about the beautiful pink colour and pattern. At one stage, I'd worried that she would ask me to knit one for her because I knew I would struggle with that decision. But she hadn't and I had breathed a sigh of relief.

Since Gill spoke to Hannah, she's been much nicer towards me and there's been a more relaxed atmosphere in the office which is good.

It's just after eight and I'm pulling on my parker jacket in the hall to head out to work when an envelope pops through letterbox. I pick it up from the mat and stare at the cream stationary and spidery handwriting. I frown. It's not a bill and I re-read the address just in case the postie has put it through the wrong door. But no, it is addressed to me with the correct flat number.

This could be from the contact centre I realise and begin to feel my knees tremble. I stagger back through to the lounge and drop down on the sofa. Is it more information about my mother? It might be bad news and something that I can't bear to hear? Or, she might have refused contact with me. I bite my lip.

I take a few deep breaths and with trembling hands I gingerly open the envelope. There is one sheet of cream paper from a notepad neatly folded. It's unusual to receive a handwritten letter nowadays because our communications all seem to be texts, emails, and voice messages on mobiles.

I take in a huge breath then let it out slowly. I open the note and read.

The words are from my mother, Mary, but they seem to be swimming all over the page. I rub my eyes to try and focus better then I gasp. My mind is in a complete whirl. My heart is galloping along at a rate of knots and sweat forms on my brow. I feel too hot and drag my thick parker off the back of my shoulders then swallow hard.

My jacket reminds me I should be heading out to work but I shake my head. I can't go there today. I need to think about what Mary has said in this letter and I pull my mobile out of the pocket.

I text a message to Gill. 'Sorry, but I've got a dodgy stomach today, so I won't be coming into work.'

I read my mother's words again and her final sentence that she would like to meet. I feel a mixture of elation and confusion. I bring a shaking hand to my forehead and start to rock gently backwards and forwards feeling completely overwhelmed. I know I must concentrate on the revelation in front of my eyes. I look at how she has signed the note, and her name, Mary.

It's an old-fashioned name which makes me wonder exactly how old she is? And, how old she had been when I was born? Quickly doing the maths I figure, if she were eighteen to twenty when she abandoned me, she would fifty-three to fifty-five now. Maybe her mother just liked the name, Mary or perhaps it is a hereditary family name. I sigh. These are the questions that have hounded me over the years knowing absolutely nothing about my parents, grandparents, and any possible siblings. I have no identity and want to know where my roots are from. I squeeze my eyes shut and wonder: am I close to solving the mystery of my birth?

Unexpected tears well up behind my eyelids and the tension in my muscle's ebbs away. I know these are feelings of a massive relief that I'm finally coming close to having my questions answered. My mother is still alive and the fact that she wants to meet makes me catch my breath. At long last I'm getting somewhere after years of hitting one brick wall after another. I have found my birth mother and she has found me. I try to sit still and let the relief sink in.

I read it once more. What does she mean trivial? I think abandoning a baby in a phone box in winter is more than blooming trivial. I swallow hard then realise that she thinks her explanations would seem trivial to me. My thoughts are jumbling up with the shock of what I have read and what is happening. I toss the note aside and stride into the kitchen to make coffee. My mouth is very dry and while waiting for the kettle to boil I gulp at a glass of cold water.

Real to her? What kind of an explanation is that? Her excuses might have felt real but what about the defenceless baby she abandoned. Did I not get a chance of living a real life, too?

I stomp back into the lounge and sit down on the sofa snatching back up the note. I read the first line; she thinks of me every day. Ha! That's a laugh, if she thought that much of me how come she never came back. She could have turned up when I was two or three begging to see me if she couldn't stop thinking about me every day.

I sip my tea and kick off my brogues. My cosy knitted slippers are tucked neatly under the coffee table and I grab at them pushing my feet inside. I'm not sure how many times I have read the note and analysed every single word that is written. I stroke the cream paper knowing my own mother has torn this out of a notepad and written these words with her pen.

It dawns upon me that in these few short sentences there is not one word of an apology. There is no begging to be forgiven. There is no lengthy explanation of why she did it. Unless, of course, she figures upon leaving her account of what happened for when we do meet. But what if I decide not to see her? Has she got a contingency plan for that eventuality?

Perhaps she's not desperate to tell me her side of the abandonment. Maybe because she has been secure in the knowledge that I was being well cared for she feels her conscience is clear.

The hours have sped by while I've been engrossed in the note. Suddenly, I need some fresh air and want to be outside. It looks very cold, but it is dry and a walk by the river might clear my thoughts. I grab my parker and handbag then hurry out of the flat.

I've walked all along the river in Durham and feel more settled in my mind about Mary's note. I look up to the splendour of our cathedral which overlooks us at every turn then climb up the steps from the riverbank onto Elvet Bridge. I turn into the marketplace to buy fruit whilst dodging between the crowds on the narrow paths.

At one of the stalls, I pick up a handful of satsumas then squeeze one of them hard in my hand. I'm beginning to feel more anger towards my mother and her few choice sentences. It doesn't appear as though she has suffered at all during my lifetime. I grimace. This is so unfair, and I want her to suffer like I've done. I want her to feel the pain and upset that I have lived through. I want her to know how it feels to be bullied and tormented all her life with no family to support her.

I realise I've squashed the satsuma so hard that juice is running through my hand and my fingers are sticky.

The market stall holder shouts at me, 'You'll have to pay for that!'

I apologise and pay for the fruit then wearily head back home. My earlier elation at receiving the letter seems to have deserted me and a cold hard resentment fills my being.

Chapter Five

Deirdre

Once home again, I head straight into the lounge and the shelving unit in the corner. I find an old notelet card with an envelope. It is pink and meant to be used for a thank you note, but as I don't possess writing paper and envelopes, I shrug my shoulders knowing this will have to do.

I decide to compose my reply to Mary as she had addressed her note to me. I frown. It's not necessary to give her any information about myself and decide to make it a simple invitation.

Wandering home from the market, I decided to ask her for tea at my flat. I have a feeling that out of the two of us I may be the only one to get upset. If this is so, I'll feel more comfortable in my own territory. I would be mortified to sit blubbering in a stranger's house. Because after all, my mother, Mary, is a stranger.

On the back of a magazine, I scribble out the few words I want to write as a practise piece and re-read the note. I nod my head deciding it is brief and a simple invitation with no explanations or welcoming words. I swallow hard. I'd like to pour my heart out and shout and scream at the unfairness of what she did. I take a deep breath knowing this could scare her off our meeting. And meet we must. I have waited a long time for this contact and the answers to my questions.

Satisfied with the note, I place it into the envelope and apply a stamp then hurry out to the corner of the street to catch the afternoon post. I figure Mary will receive this tomorrow which will give her three days to prepare herself for Sunday tea.

Returning to the lounge, I pull out the red A4 folder I have kept for years. I have copies from all the news articles I'd found in the library dated December 1985 and spread them all over the coffee table.

I stare at one clipping with the photograph of the big duffle bag in which I was found. It's white with a thistle on the front and I've often wondered if it meant that I was born in Scotland. Is that where my beginnings were or was it simply a holiday bag which Mary owned. Did she live in Durham, or had she taken a trip to bonny Scotland when she was pregnant?

I gulp. It seems different now thinking of her with a name as opposed to looking at the cuttings which state she was a nameless woman. In my thoughts she is now Mary. I still don't know anything much about her but at least she has a name.

I stare at my photograph which is my first as a baby, but how old am I? Was this taken when I was three, five, or seven days old? I have a certificate which is heart-breaking when I read it.

It says I was born on or about the 16th December. I sigh, was this at night or during the day. And where did I spend the first few hours or days of my life? I look at the photograph and wonder who had loved, fed, and kept me warm until that day. Was it Mary? Or nuns in a shelter? Perhaps a grandmother? A sister? But who?

In the columns for mother and father it states, unknown. Religion is also unknown. The birthplace column states, child found exposed.

I shiver. The word exposed always make me feel cold and unprotected somehow. I trace a finger over my name on the certificate, and wonder: did Mary give me another name before she dumped me? Perhaps there was a broken bond between us when I was born.

I stare at the baby clothes I am wearing in the photograph and recognise the knitting as a simple straightforward pattern. I can tell they have been hand-knitted and are not shop bought. Did Mary knit the cardigan, hat, and booties? And is this something Mary and I would have in common. An interest we both share and could build upon going forwards. But do I want to move forwards with her. Anger bubbles up in my chest and I clench my fists. There's many things I'd like to do to her which unfortunately are not very pleasant at all.

I shudder and realise I'm jumping ahead with my thoughts. It's silly to think we'd have anything more in common other than the normal mother and daughter bond which was obviously shattered at my birth.

Needing to do something constructive I dig into my big wool tub in the corner of the lounge and pull out two balls of white double-knit wool. I decide to copy the baby garments in the photograph that I'm wearing. I choose the correct size ten and eight needles from my knitting box and cast on the stitches for the size of a baby up to six months.

My eyes fill with tears as I quickly complete the rib on the back of the cardigan. It looks tiny. The wool feels baby-soft and squashy while I continue to stare at my photograph. How could she leave me? I've never been lucky enough to be pregnant and give birth, but I know a tiny baby that would fit into this cardigan would be so vulnerable and in need of protection. Not an exposure to the outside world in winter.

Already I am conjuring up an image of Mary in my mind. She must have been a cold and unfeeling woman to do what she did. She cannot have had one iota of motherly instinct inside her being. Which begs the question: as a woman, if you don't have the maternal instinct why have the baby in the first place? There's always contraception and if mistakes happen, terminations or adoption. If I had been adopted by Sheila and Jack it would have felt more normal. I would have coped much better with this upbringing rather than being a foundling.

I raise an eyebrow. Someone must have cared enough to knit this clothing for my birth. Perhaps a grandmother? Or an aunt? There again, I shrug my shoulders, Mary could simply have bought the things in a charity shop.

Later in the evening, I lie in bed reading the last two chapters of my Stephen King novel where a man is strangled with fishing twine on a boat. I relish in the gruesome nature of the murder and feel justified that the criminal had finally got his comeuppance.

Would I like to see Mary get her comeuppance? It's true that people would say she is not a criminal, but I see her as one. She committed an act that is against the law and should be made to pay somehow or other. The grisly fascination I have in crime and horror stories makes me frown. And, as a victim to Mary's crime, I can relate to the characters feeling of revenge.

I hold a length of strong red Aran wool between my hands and pull it firmly. It's a good bold colour and her blood will not be as obvious on the red as it would be on white or cream. I decide the Aran is strong enough and won't snap like double knitting wool might. I could wind it around Mary's neck and strangle the apologies out of her until she begs forgiveness for abandoning me. My heart begins to pump and my muscles tingle with all my senses heightened.

I hurry over to the doorway in the hall and bend forwards with the wool taught in my hands. It would make a good tripwire so when Mary walks into the lounge she will fall flat on her face, and I could tie her to the radiator with the same wool. I bounce from one slipper to another at the thought of her terrified face.

I test the points of my size 12 needles sticking out of my knitting box. Hmm, I decide, these are good and sharp to stick into her if she refuses to speak. I may have to succumb to torture on a serious level to get the information I need. Maybe a quick jab to her throat? Or a clear stab straight through her heart?

Then I wake up screaming and sweating at the nightmare I've just had and sit bolt upright in bed. My memory of the dream is as clear as if it had happened for real. I shake my head at the absurd imaginings and pull the quilt over myself. This meeting with Mary is certainly going to be a challenge, I think as I doze back off to sleep.

Chapter Six

Mary

I hadn't expected such a quick reply but when I potter downstairs in the morning and a small pink envelope is wedged in the letterbox, I somehow know it is from my daughter. I love saying the words, my daughter, now. The words are coming many years too late in my life but all the same I love to think of her. I smile turning the envelope over in my hands. It feels as precious as the crown jewels. The pink envelope and notepaper make me think she is artistic in some way. Most people would buy simple white plain stationary but obviously not my Deirdre, I smile.

I make a cup of tea and settle myself into the fireside chair to read her response. I take a deep breath. Although I know she was the one to request contact she still could have changed her mind and not want to meet. Prepare yourself for the worst, I think, and anything more will be a bonus.

Hello, Mary,

I have waited such a long time to find you and at last here you are. Yes, I'd like us to meet and if it is okay with you, I'll make tea in my flat on Sunday at 3pm.

Here is my mobile number if you cannot make this date and time. If I don't hear back from you, I will expect to see you on Sunday,

Your daughter, Deirdre

Well, it is short with the same greeting that I'd used on my letter. I'm not sure what I expected but there is no more information in the three sentences she's written other than to say how long she has waited to make contact. However, I hadn't overly written my note to her either because I want to explain everything to her in person.

I pull my shoulders back and feel a shiver run down my back. But at least I had told her that I thought about her every day. I drape my mam's old shawl around my shoulders. It still hangs over the back of the chair which is where she sat in front of the coal fire we'd had. I have a gas fire in its place now which belts out more heat but feeling Mam's shawl on my shoulders takes me back to my childhood. I remember Dad with his black face sitting in the old tin bath in front of the fire while Mam poured hot water over his hair to wash out the coal dust from the pit.

A rattle of hailstones on the window startles me and I look out at the bleak January morning. Small flakes of snow now begin to fall.

I smile knowing exactly where the modern block of flats is where Deirdre now lives. I decide to take a taxi on Sunday when I go for tea. I haven't been anywhere near that area since the day I left her in 1985 and know it's going to be heart wrenching. The flats are just behind the corner of the street where I'd hidden then sank to my knees in despair. However, I sigh, this is something I need to do for my daughter. And for myself.

I make some toast lavished with butter and marmalade and a fresh cup of tea. I shiver again but this time it is with excitement. I am longing to see her and feel a lightness creep around my stomach and up into my chest. Although, I sigh, that could be the result of the butter, of which I'm not supposed to eat much. But I prefer to think it is eagerness to finally see Deirdre.

I wonder if she will look like me and have any of our family resemblance? Her eyes had been bright blue, but all babies are at first and I wonder if they changed.

The day the midwife placed her into my arms my aunt had cried, 'Oh, Mary, she has your mam's eyes!'

I'd been so traumatised and exhausted that her words hadn't meant anything but now I remember them clearly. After my stay in the institution my memories of those six months had been vague. Even now there are large gaps I cannot remember but every now and then little snippets or sentences come back to me. I frown knowing the mind is a powerful thing.

Deirdre could of course, look like her father. This thought makes me purse my lips. In some way, I hope she doesn't because he didn't have any input into her life, well, apart from the initial conception. And, I know I have had no input either but at least I brought her into the world. The long-lost professor wouldn't know if she was dead or alive.

There is a niggle in the back of my mind telling me that up until a week ago, I didn't either, but I shrug this thought aside and hobble across to Mam's old bureau. I can't really remember exactly what he looked like, but I rummage around until I find a battered white envelope. I slide my fingers inside and pull out the old photograph of Michael.

He is wearing a green jumper and brown corduroys. His brown glasses look very old-fashioned now, but he did only wear them for reading. It was taken in the canteen by a would-be photography student who had left it lying on the table when Michael had gone. I'd slid it into the pocket of my overall when nobody was looking.

I stare at his face now and gasp at the memories. How I had kissed those lips over and over again until I'd felt quite dizzy with love for him. I had forgotten how tall he was, well over six foot with huge feet and very big hands. He is holding two books and I remember how strong and firm those hands were as he'd lovingly caressed my body. I shiver again and pull the shawl further around my shoulders then slip the photograph back into the envelop and into my handbag. I decide to take it on Sunday because Deirdre might want to look at him.

 I sit at my machine and turn on the radio knowing I must finish Elsie's dress today. As I sew, I wonder about Deirdre and her life. Is she married and do I have grandchildren? Does she have an occupation? What is her personality like? Are her foster parents still alive, and if they are, I would like to meet them. If nothing more than to thank them for raising and caring for her. There is a great deal of questions to answer on both our behalves and I pray to God she will accept my explanations of why I did what I did. I take a deep breath and determine to keep my mood happy and light. I am finally going to meet my daughter and I hug myself in anticipation.

Chapter Seven

Deirdre

I'm just about to leave work on Friday when Gill creeps up behind me. I feel her hand on my shoulder and I spin around to face her.

'I just wanted to say I hope Sunday tea with your mother goes well.'

I had told Gill all about the letter when I'd gone back to work midweek, and we discussed it at length in her office.

I feel the knots in my stomach do somersaults again then breath in and out slowly. 'Me too,' I say. 'I feel sick every time I think about her arriving to the flat and I'm beginning to regret asking her. Maybe I should have arranged to meet her in Durham in a café or somewhere?'

Gill shakes her head firmly. She takes one of my hands in hers and squeezes it tightly. 'No, Deirdre, you're doing the right thing. You both need peace and space to be able to talk,' she says. 'And you don't want everyone in Costa coffee to hear all your conversation, do you?'

I nod my head knowing she is right. 'I just wish I didn't feel so nervous and hyped up about meeting her.'

'Well, that's perfectly normal after all the years you've waited. And remember what we talked about the other day? Mary will feel just as anxious as you do if not more so because she was the one who walked away.'

I nod and try a half smile. 'Yep, I've got that,' I say and push my arm through the sleeve of my parker. I chant the next sentence, 'Take deep breaths and stay calm.'

Gill grins and pulls the jacket over my shoulder almost as if she were dressing a child. 'God, I'm so excited for you and can't wait to hear all about it on Monday.'

I smile at the sparkle in her eyes and can see she truly means her well wishes. I think of all the support and encouragement she has given me on my journey and take her arm as we walk out of the office together.

'I don't know how to thank you for everything you've done, Gill,' I say. 'I…I mean, well without you, I would never have got this far!'

She turns to me and gives me a quick hug. 'Of course, you would,' she says. 'It probably would have taken a while longer, but you'd definitely have done it. Now, if you've time on Sunday night for a brief text that would be great but if not, I'll see you Monday.'

She strides off into the car park calling good luck over her shoulder and I amble down the drive and onto the pavement heading for home.

***

It's two o'clock on Sunday afternoon and I'm pacing around my flat like a caged animal. It is here. The day has arrived. I am finally going to meet my mother. Will we be able to make up for lost time? I don't know and frown. Maybe when I meet her, I won't want to make up with her. I might not like what I see. She could be the last person on earth that I would like to get to know. I eye the red wool in the basket and remember my dream. This could be something I actually put into practise, I think, and begin to tremble.

I've had three different outfits on, and none seemed appropriate. I'd groaned in front of the long bedroom mirror. What do you wear to greet a mother you have never seen before?

I tried on a dark green dress which I bought for a wedding last year but cast it aside deciding it looked frumpy and old fashioned. Then I tried to pull up new jeans that were bought at Christmas, but they were so tight I could hardly breathe. I'd peeled and unravelled them down my legs and sat on the bed close to tears.

I wanted to look nice, and dare I think, even confident in my appearance but my mood has slumped now. And this is all her fault. My bloody mother. She's to blame for my lack of self-confidence, I moan, then pull on an old pair of black leggings and a brown Fair Isle sweater.

I stride into the bathroom and pull at the tufts in my cropped brown hair. Usually, I wet it on a morning, and it seems to stick up which I think is a trendy style but today this doesn't happen. I try some oil on the ends of the tufts but now it looks like I have been plugged into a socket and electrocuted. Sweeping a small amount of blusher across my cheeks I then apply a pale pink lipstick and hope for the best.

I begin to pace from room to room. Mary will be the first person who has ever been inside my flat. In one way, I decide it will be a chance to show off my hard work at designing the rooms, but in another way, it feels scary as though I'm allowing an intruder inside my safe haven. Chaining her to the radiator pops back into my mind and I take a deep breath. I mustn't let all the anger and hatred pour out of me before I get my answers.

  I stride into the kitchen and double check the scones and cake I have prepared for tea. The plates are on the bench ready to carry through to the lounge with the small teapot and cups. I run my hands back and forth along the edge of the bench hoping that she likes lemon cake. What if she doesn't? My stomach lurches as I don't have an alternative to offer. Perhaps I should have bought a chocolate cake as a standby?

  I take a deep breath and hurry through to the lounge. I fluff up the two cream cushions on the sofa which don't need it and then open the slats on the blinds to peer outside. It is bitterly cold and has been sleeting this morning, but this appears to have stopped now. I look up at the sky which is simply grey and dismal.

How will she get here? Will she whizz up in a fancy big car like Gill has? Most fifty-year olds drive nowadays. In fact, I think I am the only woman in Durham that never learnt to drive and walks everywhere. I look at the space in the car park that is allocated to my flat and hope she will realise that is where she can leave her car.

At exactly three o'clock, I watch from behind the blinds to see if she approach's the front of the flats. This way, I'll be able to look at her before she arrives and sees me.

Forewarned is forearmed, as Shirley would say. I think of her and wonder if she would have been glad that I was finally meeting my birth mother. I perch on the end of the sofa and pick at the skin on my thumb. I decide she probably would. For as long as I can remember she had always wanted the best for me and had been totally open about my beginnings from the start. I think she would also like answers to the questions too. I know from her comments over the years, she struggled with the fact that a woman could leave her baby unprotected.

I sigh and glance at the clock. Another ten minutes to wait. I feel like I am sitting in the dreaded dentist waiting room.

Chapter Eight

Deirdre

A gentle tap on the door makes me shoot up from the sofa. My heart begins to thump, and I rush to the window. There is no car parked but I see the back of a taxi pull away.

I hurry along the hall. Damn, I'd never thought of her arriving in a taxi. I stand behind the door squeezing my clammy hands together. I look at the corners of the skirting boards and wish I'd prepared the red wool as a trip wire. I'd like to see her fall flat on her face. My cheeks burn and I take a deep breath. This is it. My mother is on the other side of this door.

I wipe the palms of my hands down my leggings and slowly open the door.

I gasp. There is an old lady standing in front of me and I know my mouth has dropped open. I stare at her and then look past her shoulder. Maybe Mary has brought a friend or her mother with her - is this my grandmother?

'Hello, Deirdre,' she says. 'I'm your mother, Mary.'

My thoughts are racing trying to piece this together. I realise I'm keeping her standing at the doorway, but I can only manage to stammer, 'A…Are you?'

She nods and steps towards me as I open the door wider. She walks into my hall, and I close the door behind her.

I lick my dry lips. 'But you're old?'

She nods. 'Yes, I suppose I am now that I've reached my seventieth birthday.'

I know I have been very rude and mumble an apology, 'Sorry, it's just that, well…' I look down at the floor. 'I'd expected you to be much younger.'

I look up again and she smiles. I recognise the shape of my mouth and lips from looking in the mirror. I can see the resemblance in her eyes, too.

I shake myself and usher her through to the lounge.

She is rubbing her hands together in smart black leather gloves. 'Goodness, it's really cold today.'

I nod as though I'm struck dumb and stare at her tailored red coat. I decide this is where our likeness ends because she is petite and looks just over five foot tall. Her grey hair is neatly trimmed around her small face, and she has tiny bird-like hands that seem to flutter as she removes her gloves. There is nothing ungainly about this woman and I can tell there never has been.

She unbuttons the large black buttons down the front of her coat. I step towards her as she removes it from her shoulders.

'I'll just hang this up,' I say and move back into the hall. 'Please have a seat.'

I hold the coat to my body and sway slightly in front of the coat pegs. My mind is in a whirl. She is seventy, so I reckon this would have made her thirty-five when she gave birth.

The same age as I am now. Is that a coincidence or not? The wool coat smells of a light flowery fragrance and it makes me smile. I pull my shoulders back knowing it is not Mary's fault that I am shocked about her age. I have obviously calculated and misjudged the situation completely. I'd naturally thought, as Gill and Sheila had, that Mary must have been very young and rash to abandon her baby, but obviously not.

I take a deep breath and head back into the lounge.

Mary hasn't sat down but is wandering around the walls looking at the framed pictures I've hung. 'These are lovely scenes, Deirdre. I can tell you have an artistic flair.'

I smile and stand behind her. 'Yes, I bought them from a local artist who has a stall down in the marketplace. The painting of our cathedral in the snow is my favourite.'

Mary stares at it intently and nods. 'It's beautiful and I can see why you like it so much,' she says.

She turns and sits on the sofa then looks up at me as I stand in front of her. 'It's special, just like you are.'

I gulp. I hadn't expected to launch into talking about us so quickly and my cheeks flush at her words. 'I'll pop the kettle on,' I say. 'A cup of tea will warm you up.'

She nods and I hurry behind her into the kitchen. My hands are trembling as I boil the kettle and pick up the two plates to carry though into the lounge. I drop them back down onto the bench and grasp my hands together to try and stop them trembling.

This changes everything. When I'd thought Mary was in her fifties, I had planned to verbally attack her for dumping me and wrecking my life. But now, I sigh, I cannot rant at an elderly lady. Maybe other people could but that is not the way Sheila raised me. I have too much respect for my elders to berate and upset her.

I take a few more deep breaths. In a louder voice through the open plan area Mary tells me all about her taxi ride to get here and what the driver had been saying about her village.

I feel steadier and pick up the plates once more then carry them through. She has settled back into the sofa in her green dress that hangs just below her knees. I note her thin short legs and small feet in black leather ankle boots. She has a good dress sense and I decide the green outfit she is wearing looks expensive.

'Oh, Deirdre, how lovely. Lemon cake is my favourite.'

I cannot help but smile remembering my previous concerns which don't exist now.

'Mine too,' I call over my shoulder heading back to the kitchen.

I make a few trips with the teapot and cups then small plates, milk, and sugar.

'Now, that's great, Deirdre,' she says. 'We already have a snowy cathedral and lemon cake in common.'

I let her pour the tea because that's what mothers do, isn't it? I smile watching her munch into a slice of cake and licking her lips.

'Are you a bit warmer now, Mary?'

She nods and smiles. 'Oh, yes, thank you. And, unless I'm mistaken this is a M&S lemon cake, Deirdre?'

I notice she uses my name a lot which pleases me. A little like I have done since I found out her name. 'It is from M&S, Mary because I think they make the best lemon cake ever!'

I nibble at a scone, but the texture feels dry in the back of my mouth, and I gulp at the tea. I know we must start talking soon and not about the cake, but I am not sure how to start.

Mary takes this quandary away as I watch her finish her tea then take a white lace handkerchief from the sleeve of her dress and dab at her mouth. 'So, if it's okay with you, Deirdre, I'm going to tell you all about us and what happened.'

I gulp and nod. Now that it is here, I brace myself for the disclosure of my birth. The panicky part of my mixed-up mind can hear Sheila say, 'Ignorance is bliss, or be careful what you wish for.'

Mary rests her head back on the sofa and closes her eyes then starts to tell me about her life in the village, her parents, her sewing skills, and her sheltered upbringing until she met my father, the professor.

I am entranced. I am staring at her and listening to every word of the story. I am terrified that I miss one tiny piece. I can feel my heart speed up as she talks about being sent up to Edinburgh where I was born on the 13th December. Then she talks about the train journey home and how scared she was when she got off the train at Durham station and I was howling.

Suddenly she sits forwards and puts her hands over her face. Tears are running through her fingers. I stare at the old wrinkly skin on her hands and my heart melts.

I slide off the opposite chair and kneel in front of her squeezing her arms. 'It's okay,' I say. 'Take a breather, Mary.'

'No,' she says and chokes back a sob. 'Y…You have a right to know, and I have to tell you this now.'

I'm stunned as I listen to how she'd left me in the telephone box and waited on the corner of the street until she saw a woman rescue me. She cannot remember what happened after that but tells me about the psychiatric hospital. She tells me about the ECT treatment for what they now call post-natal depression, and a shiver runs up my back. I know exactly where St. Margaret's is in the city although I have never been inside. I shudder to think what it was like thirty-five years ago.

She removes her hands and dries her face with the lace handkerchief then rests her head back on the sofa. She looks pale and worn out then closes her eyes again.

I rock back on my heels. I have blamed and hated this woman all my life. In my mind I have wanted to do evil horrible things to make her suffer. I remember the dream with the vivid images of the strong wool, tripwire, and sharp pointed needles.

I shrug my shoulders and can see in her eyes that she has probably suffered as much as I have. I slip back up onto the sofa and think through everything she's told me about herself and her lifestyle. It's impossible to think in these days that a woman of thirty-five would still be a virgin and get pregnant through ignorance. But, I suppose, in 1985 living in a small village with little wherewithal it would have been entirely plausible.

My shoulders relax and my whole posture slumps back into the soft seat. So that is it. That is my story. These were my beginnings in life. I let out a huge breath. Now at least I know.

I look at Mary who seems to have dozed off to sleep. I think of waking her, but she has a peaceful look on her face. She must feel relieved now to get her story out in the open. My mouth is dry, and I get up on wobbly legs then head into the kitchen to make fresh tea. I clean the cups and refill the teapot glad of little things to do for distraction.

When I return to the lounge Mary sits up startled. 'Oh dear, I must have dozed off,' she says. 'How rude of me coming to visit and fall asleep.'

'That doesn't matter,' I say. 'I've made some fresh tea. I think we could do with a strong cup.'

We talk and talk and talk. I admire her dress and claim that I struggle to even sew on a button. Mary compliments me on my jumper and confesses to never learning how to knit. I tell her all about Sheila and she listens with great interest but is upset to learn of their deaths in the accident.

Mary asks, 'And, you've been alone since then?'

I nod. For some reason I find Mary incredibly easy to talk to about my life. I pour my heart out to her, which for me is a first. I tell her about my engagement and about Hannah calling me the weirdo at work.

'You see, I've never made friends easily. The women I work with are my only contacts now, but I wouldn't call them friends, other than Gill, of course. And there is a part of me that can't trust anyone anymore. I feel as though my background has stopped me from doing this,' I say. A big lump gathers in the back of my throat, but I push on, 'I've put barriers up to protect myself because no one else ever would. I've never had any family to do this for me like other people have.'

I see Mary's eyes swim with tears. 'Dear God, this is my fault,' she says. 'I've done this to you, Deirdre.'

I watch her look past me and focus on our snowy cathedral painting. 'My mam was cruel with her tongue and for years after I came out of St. Margaret's she told everyone I was unhinged! I knew I wasn't but agreeing with her was easier than arguing. So, when I thought of you back then I'd figured giving you away to someone else was the best thing I could have done for you. But I can see now that I was wrong,' she mutters. 'I was wrong, so very wrong.'

She looks down at her hands in her lap. 'I'm terribly sorry...'

I shake my head. 'No, Mary, I've always blamed you for the way I am but I'm just beginning to realise that I did have choices growing up. And I still do,' I say. 'So, I think a lot of this is my own fault.'

I look up again and pull my shoulders back then try to be more positive. 'Okay, tell me more about Edinburgh.'

She tells me every snippet she can remember about my birth and her old aunt in the big Scottish townhouse. 'She's still alive now at the age of ninety-one,' Mary says. 'And I have two cousins both in their early seventies that live near her. I don't see them now, but we still exchange Christmas and birthday cards.'

I nod with interest to learn that at least I have some family albeit in an older age group. I am beginning to judge Mary's character now and am pleased she is not like my grandmother who sounded cruel. Mary seems loving and caring and such a gentle soul that I'm not surprised a man took advantage of her sensitive nature.

She is staring at my face now and leans across to gently lay her hand on my cheek. 'There's just a certain way you have of turning your head that reminds me of him,' she says, and lifts her handbag up from the floor.

I raise an eyebrow and watch her pull out a tatty old envelope. 'Do you want to know about your father?'

A flutter begins way down in my stomach, and I gasp. 'W…well, I'm not altogether sure,' I say and swallow hard. 'He has never really figured much in my thoughts over the years, it has always been about you.'

She nods, 'Well, maybe enough is enough for one day. I do have a photograph of him, but you could always look some other time.'

I stare at the ragged corner of the photograph sticking out of the envelope and know I must see him. I lick my dry lips.

'Yes!' I almost shout and I can see I've startled Mary. 'I mean, yes please, I'd like to see him.'

Mary slides the photograph out of the envelope and hands it to me. 'Of course, as I told you before all I know is that he transferred to a university in Wales, and I never heard from him.'

The first thing I notice about the man who was my father, is how tall he is and the size of his huge feet and hands. I smile, no doubt this is who I take after. He is the parent I must blame for my cumbersome body.

He is smiling into the camera and instantly I can see what Mary fell in love with. He has an air of self-containment about him. A look of a leader who is confident in his attitude and position in the university. I hold the photograph closer and read aloud the name badge pinned to his shirt, 'Professor Michael Davidson.'

'Yes, that's him,' Mary says, and leans closer to look over my shoulder. 'He was a handsome devil if I say so myself.'

My mind is spinning again. It should be quite easy to find him through university documents although he will be retired now or could even have died.

I smile then ask, 'Was he the same age as you, Mam?'

Mary gasps and I realise I've just called her Mam. I put my fingers over my mouth and stare at her. 'Sorry, I…I, well,' I stumble over my words.

The grin spreads right across her face. 'Oh, Deirdre, my long-lost darling daughter. Please don't be sorry. It was lovely to hear you say that word. To call me your mam was the best thing I've ever heard.'

I grin back at her. 'And I loved saying it, too.'

She turns towards me, and I see her eyes are full of tears now. She mutters, 'Can you ever forgive me?'

I inch further towards her on the sofa and the photograph flutters to the floor. She holds her arms out and I slide into her embrace. We hug each other and I don't want to let go.

All my questions are answered. Now I know exactly who I am. I know how I was born and where it had been. I can't judge her for abandoning me because I've never felt unbalanced in my state of mind like she had been. And fortunately, I've never had to stay in a psychiatric hospital nor had post-natal depression. But I can at least understand those reasons.

She is tiny and frail in my arms. I feel her rub my back in slow movements. My shoulders slump and I let everything go. All the hurt and anger towards her leaves me.

I am not sure about forgiveness and why she didn't try to find me when she was well again, but perhaps that will be something we can work on together.

I smile. Finally, I feel at peace with myself.

Chapter Nine

Mary

I settle back into the seat of the taxi and take a deep breath. I can't seem to stop grinning. I have met my daughter and she is a lovely young lady. An accomplished knitter and has an artistic flair which is apparent in the way she has designed her home. She has a good steady job although I don't care for the women in the office, other than Gill of course, who I would like to meet and thank for her help.

Deirdre has accepted me for who I am and, why I abandoned her at the time. I know it will take a while for us to work through the following years when I didn't contact her, and I frown. This will always be something I bitterly regret. If only I'd had more confidence to contact her then we would have had years of enjoyment together. But now our time is going to be limited.

I haven't told her about the pancreatic cancer which I know was a little cowardly. But we were having such a lovely time together and I hadn't wanted to put a dampener on everything. Our conversation had been better than I could ever have hoped for. I'd decided before I went that the worst thing that could have happened would have been the door shutting in my face. Which, to be honest, I would have totally understood.

I will certainly tell her next weekend when she plans to visit me in my cottage. I will have a whole week to decided how to explain the diagnosis and what the doctors have advised.

Strangely enough it is a diagnosis that is not wholly surprising to me. Since my dad died of stomach cancer, I've somehow known that I would follow in his footsteps and how I wouldn't reach my eighties. In fact, I think the doctors will be surprised if I live to see another Christmas.

I lay my head back against the seat and curse silently under my breath. What an awful time for it to happen just as I get my daughter back into my life. God certainly moves in mysterious ways.

Printed in Great Britain
by Amazon

58765858R00046